THIS CANDLEWICK BOOK BELONGS TO:

_____

_____

_____

_____

For
Michael John

J.C.

For
Mum and Dad

S.L.

Text copyright © 1993 by June Crebbin
Illustrations copyright © 1993 by Stephen Lambert

All rights reserved.

First U.S. paperback edition 1995

Library of Congress Cataloging-in-Publication Data

Crebbin, June.
Fly by night / June Crebbin; illustrated by Stephen Lambert. — 1st U.S. ed.

Summary: A young owl eagerly awaits the nighttime
to make his first flight with his mother.
1. Owls—Juvenile fiction. [1. Owls—Fiction. 2. Flight—Fiction.]
I. Lambert, Stephen, 1964– ill. II. Title.
PZ10.3.C859Fl   1993   [E]—dc20   92-53140
ISBN 1-56402-149-1 (hardcover)—ISBN 1-56402-508-X (paperback)

2 4 6 8 10 9 7 5 3 1

Printed in Hong Kong

The pictures in this book were done in chalk pastel.

Candlewick Press
2067 Massachusetts Avenue
Cambridge, Massachusetts 02140

FLY BY NIGHT

June Crebbin

illustrated by Stephen Lambert

CANDLEWICK PRESS
CAMBRIDGE, MASSACHUSETTS

Once, at the edge of the woods, lived two owls, a mother owl and her young one, Blink. Every day, all day long, they slept. Every night, all night long, the mother owl flew and Blink waited.

One day,
when the sun
was still low in the sky, Blink opened
one eye and said, "Now? Is it time?"
"Soon," said his mother. "Soon.
Go back to sleep."

Blink tried
to sleep.

When the sun rose and warmed the earth,
he opened the other eye. "*Now* is it time?"
"Not yet," said his mother. "Soon.
Go back to sleep."

Blink tried.

Butterflies looped and drifted

past him. Beetles scuttled in the

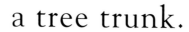

undergrowth. Nearby, a

woodpecker tapped on

a tree trunk.

Blink couldn't sit still.

"Is it time *yet?*" he said.

His mother opened her eyes.

"You are old enough and strong

enough . . . "—Blink dithered with

excitement—"but you must wait."

His mother closed her eyes.

"Wait for *what?*" Blink wondered.

The sun was at its highest.
A squirrel leapt from tree to
tree, quicker than a thought.
Along Blink's branch it came,
right past him, its tail
streaming out behind.
Blink wriggled and jiggled.
He *couldn't* sit still.

 All that long
afternoon,
he watched and
waited. He shuffled and fidgeted.
Below, in the clearing, a deer and
its fawn browsed on leaves and twigs.
High above, a falcon hovered, dipped,
and soared again into the sky.
"When will it be *my* time?" said
Blink to himself.

Toward dusk, a sudden gust
of wind, sweeping through
the woods, lifting leaves on
their branches, seemed to
gather Blink from his branch
as if it would lift him too.
"Time to fly," it seemed to say.
Blink fluffed out his feathers.
He shifted his wings.

But the wind swirled by.

It was all puff and nonsense.

Blink sighed. He closed his eyes.

The sun slipped behind the fields.

The moon rose pale and clear.

A night breeze stirred. "Time to fly."

"Puff and nonsense," muttered Blink.

"*Time to fly*," said his mother beside him.

Blink sat up. "Is it?"

he said. "Is it? *Really?*"

The gray dusk had deepened.

Blink heard soft whisperings.

He saw the stars in the sky.

He felt the dampness of the

night air. He knew it was

time to fly. He gathered his

strength. He drew himself up.

He stretched out his wings and—

lifted into the air. Higher and higher.

He flew. Farther and farther. Over the woods, over the fields, over the road

and the sleeping city. High in the sky, his wing beats strong, Blink flew on.

Now he knew what he'd been waiting for.

The sun had slipped behind the fields,
the stars had appeared in the night sky.

He had waited because he was meant to

fly by night.

JUNE CREBBIN wrote this story after she found an owl at the bottom of a tree at a school near her house. "There was a party going on, and right on the edge of all this activity was an owl sitting very happily. It inspired me." June Crebbin is also the author of *Danny's Duck*, illustrated by Clara Vulliamy.

STEPHEN LAMBERT says the text for this book appealed to him right away "because it's the kind of story I would like to have written myself." Stephen Lambert is also the illustrator of June Crebbin's *The Train Ride*, as well as *What Is the Sun?* by Reeve Lindbergh.